Titanic II: The

A

By Darrell Wright (darrelld713@gmail.com)

Summary:

A sequel to *Titanic*. Through her diary, found after her death, much more is learned about things that Rose Dawson had kept in her heart during her life. After being rescued at sea, Rose lives in New York several years, goes to California, then to Wisconsin where she meets Jack Dawson's relatives, learns much more about Jack, and marries his cousin Jeremy, who is apparently murdered by her ex-fiance Caledon's men. Rose moves to Milwaukee and marries Darrell Calvert. Rose dreams often of Jack and feels his presence in her life. Jack helps Rose in various mysterious ways during her life, but most importantly by inspiring her to sacrifice herself for others and by gradually helping her to forgive the survivors of the Titanic for their failure to return and rescue those in the water. Other facts about Rose's life are revealed at her funeral. Story continues with events in the life of Rose's granddaughter Lizzy and her husband Brock. Authenticity of various paranormal experiences of Rose, involving Jack, at first uncertain, seems to be gradually confirmed by the end of the movie.

(Story begins with the finding of Rose dead in her bed, along with her diary beside her, among her other mementos she brought with her on the salvage boat. On the cover of the diary is an ornate heart. Her granddaughter Lizzy begins reading a letter written by to her by Rose placed on the cover of the diary.)

(Date: night of her death, 1996)

"Dear Lizzy,

I suppose you will be the one to find this diary, which I have shown to no one during my lifetime. Now that I am gone I see no reason to keep from you and the rest of the family and whoever else who may be interested, some of the things that happened both in my life and in my heart after being rescued at sea following the sinking of the Titanic. I have kept within my heart so many things, and I have been strongly tempted many times to destroy what I have written here. The only reason I did not destroy it is to help ensure that the memory of Jack Dawson, to whom I owe my life, and so much more, may never die.

"You may be thinking that I took some pills or something to end my life, but it is not so. Jack told me that this would be the night of our reunion. If after reading the diary you still find it hard to believe this, and the things that have happened in my life, especially relating to Jack, I will see if I can provide you with some sign after I depart. If I were in your shoes, I'd find it difficult to believe too! Goodbye for now, my dear. I will always be with you in a special way. And please give a kiss to everyone in the family for me.

Your loving grandmother,

Rose"

(Lizzy looks closely at the cover of the diary, then opens it.)

"4/ 19/1912"

"My heart lies at the bottom of the sea, because that is where you, my darling, are. Oh Jack, if you can hear me, I want you to know that I will never stop loving you. I do not think I could even if I tried. During the brief time we were together I finally felt for the first time that there was meaning in my life, but now it has all vanished. You not only gave me reason to live, but you opened my heart to love for the first, and possibly the last time. You also opened my eyes to what is real, to what is most important in the world and in life. But if I cannot see you again, I would rather have them closed forever. Oh, my darling, please show me in some way that you have not left me forever!"

"After my rescue from the shipwreck, I decided to abandon my family name. I did it for two reasons: because I knew deep down that I could no longer live the empty and superficial life that my mother had tried so hard to prepare me for.

(Flashback: "May I have your name, Miss?" "Dawson. Rose Dawson.")

"But primarily I did it for Jack…. After arriving in New York I knew that my mother would do all she could to find me, and most likely Caledon would as well, if not for me at least for the diamond."

(Show mother reading list of survivors)

Mrs. Bukater: Rose Dawson...O God!

(She goes to see Caledon and shows him the name on the list. He feigns interest.)

Caledon: Do you believe it could be her?

Mrs. Bukater: I don't know what to believe, but we must try to find her if it is!

Caledon: I'll put my people on it at once…If she survived, Mrs. Bukater, we will find her.

Caledon (to his father, later): Mrs Bukater thinks that "Rose Dawson" is her daughter. I told her that we would look for her.

Mr. Hockley: That's fine…It's too bad we won't be able to find her.

Caledon: Yes, it certainly is. Any woman who would take the name of that…*peasant* has not only completely lost her mind but according to any sound judgment has irretrievably lost all dignity as well.

Mr. Hockley: But we won't be finished with her until we find out if she still has the diamond.

(Flashback: Rose pulling necklace out of coat pocket, then later hiding it in her bra and dropping coat overboard)

"One of the first things I did when we landed in New York was walk out to the end of the Manhatten pier and just stare out toward the direction of where I thought Jack was. I did it every day for at least two weeks. Then after a few days of not going, I went one more time. It was then that I said:
(Show Rose on pier.)

Rose: Jack, I want to be with you. I need you to help me to go on!

"And then I saw a shooting star. A familiar voice then said…"

Molly Brown: They say that every time you see a shooting star, it's a soul going to heaven.

Rose: Oh, Molly!

(They embrace, Rose weeping, Molly comforts her, they exchange post-Titanic experiences, including…)

Molly: If I could I would have thrown every single one of those cowardly bastards out of the boat! They didn't deserve to live. And the women, they just sat there and said nothing. Some threatened to throw me overboard! It was insane!

(Molly invites Rose to stay with her, Rose declines. Molly has heard that Caledon knows of Rose being in NY, and is preoccupied with whether she has the diamond which he put in the coat pocket.)

Rose: That coat is at the bottom of the Atlantic Ocean. If you see him, you can tell him I wish him luck in finding it.

Molly: Rose, are you sure there's nothing I can do for you?

Rose: I'm sure. I'll be fine, Molly. Remember, I'm a survivor, like you.

Molly: This is my address until I go to Philadelphia next week. Please look me up, dear. It's important to me that you come. And take this (puts money in Rose's purse). I will worry myself sick and won't sleep unless you do. And this will be my address in Philadelphia.

"Even though I got off the Carpathia without the coat, I knew it wouldn't be safe if I kept the diamond necklace with me, so I buried it. My fears were confirmed when several days later I came home to my apartment and could see that someone had been there, looking through my belongings."

Caledon (to father): I don't think she has it. No one remembers her getting off the ship with the coat, and it's not in that hovel she's living in.

Mr. Hockley: Well, at least it's insured. But it would have been nice to have both the diamond *and* the insurance money.

Caledon: Yes, that would certainly have been ideal.

"Soon after I arrived in New York I got a job singing in a night club. (Show Rose in New York, singing, living in the "fast lane," etc.) I found out that the easiest way to get rid of the pain of being without Jack was to immerse myself in the noise and activity of the city, especially the night life. While involved in the night club scene I associated in general with people my mother would likely find even more offensive than Jack. I think I did it mainly as a form of rebellion against all that my mother and her world stood for, a world I was now ready to turn my back on forever. It also helped me to forget about Jack… But oftentimes when I was alone and it was quiet, I would think of him, imagine him next to me, holding me, making love to me, or just imagine us together looking into each other's eyes. And then I would usually cry, knowing that these things would never happen again. At such times I would often get the necklace, which I kept with me now though safely hidden away, and put it on. I didn't associate the diamond with Caledon anymore, but now it became the special sign of the bond between me and Jack. He would always be for me the true "heart of the sea," and my heart was still with him. The necklace became for me a symbol of our love and our connection, one that I just could not let die, even though I could only see him and hold him in my dreams and in my memory. (Show Rose standing before mirror wearing the diamond necklace, then closing her eyes and imagining Jack standing behind her, his arms around her.)

Jack: Rose Dawson, you are the loveliest woman in the world. (They kiss.)

"Sometimes I would talk to Jack as if he were really there with me. And many times when I did, it seemed like I could feel his presence. At times it was a comforting feeling, at others it was as if he were speaking to my conscience, admonishing me, urging me to be strong, encouraging me to be everything I could be, and to not lose hope. It was at those times that I would recall the promise he made me make to him before I lost consciousness in the icy waters of the Atlantic, and then lost him. (Flashback of "the promise", and of Jack sinking into the water) At other times I would try to forget about Jack, because thinking about him made me feel the pain of separation too much. I still loved him so much, so much that my heart often felt like it could not take it anymore.

"I knew deep down that living the night life of NY could be nothing more than a temporary palliative to help relieve the pain I felt inside. Ultimately it was just as unsatisfying as the life I was living before. So after a few years in NY I felt a growing desire to do some of the things that Jack said we would do together: like riding horses on the beach in California, fishing, and riding on the roller coaster. I took a train to San Francisco. And when I was doing these things that Jack talked about I felt his presence more than usual. I couldn't tell if it was all in my mind and my imagination, but it helped at least a little to soothe the pain and fill some of the emptiness I felt inside me."

(On horse: After riding for a while, Rose imagines riding double with Jack, hers arms around him, going faster than she'd like. She hears Jack say...)

"Do you trust me?" "I trust you, Jack." "Hold on!" "I'm holding on!… I'll always hold on, Jack!" "Not always. You'll know when to let go." "I'm afraid to let go!"

(Fishing: While looking out upon the sea Rose then closes her eyes and imagines walking with Jack along boat dock.)

Jack: Okay, now close your eyes. (They walk farther) Okay, open your eyes now. (Show 60' sailboat) Our Ship of Dreams, Rose. Do you like it?

Rose: Oh! It's beautiful! (They board. Show them sailing, then on the bow, then kissing while "orinoco flow" by Enya plays . Then Rose is shaken from daydream by her fishing line whizzing, as large marlin is hooked.)

(Flying plane) "I even learned how to fly. When I was in the air I would sometimes think about standing with Jack on the bow of the Titanic. (Flashback) One time I let go of the wheel as I was carried back in my mind to that moment, one still so precious to me. The plane started plunging, and then spinning out of control. Then all of a sudden it seemed like I felt hands on mine, helping me to bring the plane back under control. I felt quite sure it was Jack. And then I heard him speak to me in a dream that very night: 'Rose, after you land, begin to plant your garden.' I thought to myself, Why would Jack tell me to do that? But after a while I didn't think about it anymore.

"I remembered, of course, that Jack was from Chippewa Falls, Wisconsin (Flashback: '…are you a Boston Dawson?' 'No, I'm a Chippewa Falls Dawson'). As time went on I felt that it was my duty to go there and tell his family what happened to him, at least what they needed to know. Besides, he saved my life, and I thought it might give them some comfort to know that he did not die in vain.

"I also had a growing desire to find out more about him, to meet his relatives and others who might be able to tell me more about Jack, which I hoped would also help fill somewhat the void in my own heart."

(Rose travels to Chippewa Falls, WI, finds some of Jack's relatives, also Dawsons [they are Catholics], with whom she stays. Rose reverts to her former name Bukater. She tells them that Jack saved her life and then died of the cold, but not of their falling in love. They all show their grief, then Rose asks to be excused and steps outside. Soon Millie Dawson [Jack's aunt] joins her, puts her arm around her, then Rose hugs her, crying.)

Rose: They could have saved him and most of the others! There were 20 lifeboats, and only one came back, and that was after almost everyone was dead! They should have saved him!

Millie: Yes, they should have saved him, and others with him. But they must have also been so frightened, and confused. It's hard to say what someone would do in the same situation. But yes, they should have come back.

(The two go back inside. They tell Rose things about Jack, how he lost his parents and younger brother and sister in the flu epidemic of 1909, and show her some of his art work and also some poetry he wrote...)

Shauna (Millie's daughter): And he even mentions your name in one of them!

Mary (other daughter): He does?

Shauna: Yeah, he was in love with a girl named Rose.

Millie: We don't know that, Shauna. He may have just called her a rose, meaning the flower. And Jack didn't even know Rose at that time. Here, let me show them to you, Rose.

The Song of the Silent Swan
I came upon a swan and asked to hear from it a song;
It said, "I sing in silence, and in silence you will hear
A song far greater - if you will but listen to His voice

Whom you with earthly eyes can't see, because He is so near."

"But I am not permitted yet to sing, or I would lie:
For God made me to listen in the silence my life long,
Composing every day for Him the notes of one sweet song,
Which I will sing most beautifully the day I am to die."

Dec., 1910

Nature's Parables: Winter

We hear it very often when it's wet
 and cold: the curse, the murmur, the
 complaint;
 as if we held almighty God in debt
 to give us warmth and sunlight, and to paint
 the world bright green without the snow and
 rain;
 to send fair Summer, pleasant Fall and Spring
 without the cold and wind - without the *pain*.
 As if we did not know that would not bring
  more happiness, but total, painful loss.
 Can there be life without the winter rain?
 Can we accept its gifts and still complain?
 And do you hate the cold? It makes us strong.
We learn to love the light when nights are long -
  In Winter lives the mystery of the Cross.

Nov., 1910

Nature's Parables: Death

"Sunt lacrymae rerum et mentem mortalia tangunt"
(Virgil, Aeneid, 1, 462)

All living things fade quickly, and they die:
What is the meaning? Can we answer why?
The bird consumes a worm or scattered seed;
The day it cannot fly it will then feed
Some other creature; then it will return
To earth, enriching soil for plants in turn.
And so it is with plants and beasts - and Man
As well - yet he alone in nature can
Perceive the tragic beauty in it all -
Yet they see least who know not of their fall.

Nov., 1910

The Gift of Time

It is a mystery what we call Time:
A little space of day which turns to night;
A little span of sorrow and delight:
Of tearful dirges and of joy-bells' chime.
And yet its calm, slow-moving, noiseless feet
Can lead to glory - even thru defeat,
Enclose the wicked within their self-made bars,
And lift God-fearing souls beyond the stars!
O but foolish, blind, ungrateful souls are they
That, heedless, see no gift in each new day.

Oct., 1910

I Will Await You

"Soles occidere et redire possunt:
Nobis cum semel occidit brevis lux
Nox est perpetua una dormienda."

(Catullus, Carmina, v.)

Suns may set and suns may rise,
But our poor mortal eyes,
When their days of light are past

Will shut, and go to sleep at last.

But no, great Poet - we shall rise
Again - Yes, these my mortal eyes
Shall open once again from sleep
When my love joins me in the deep.
Dec., 1910

(Show Rose reading the above poem. She looks somewhat startled
after reading the last line.)

(Untitled)
Winnowing winds invade our lives,
They stir us in life's brief sojourn;
As groping men we must survive
Life's "slings and arrows", and must learn
That things perceived are oft' unclear:
Mind's darkness casts a shadow deep,
Which leaves us often prey to fear -
And where is rest this side of sleep?
I've found it in another's heart:
She's in my heart but not my hand;
I knew it from the very start:
She's raised me high - when shall I land?
What do I do - how much to give?
Uncertainty pervades my days;
I know we have two lives to live,
But how - together? Doubts here raise
The question deep: will we two join,
Or is it passing fancy this?
O God, life's swords are poignant -
Yet I've never known such poignant bliss.
Dec., 1910

`(Untitled)

There is no rose without a piercing thorn,
And shadow closely cleaves to radiant light;
And though for life and love we have been born,
Our life's a struggle, love our painful plight.

But you are light alone and my life's breath,
And for you daily my love tender grows;
A thousand thorns I'll challenge unto death
For you who've pierced my heart, my love, sweet Rose.

                                        Dec., 1910

(Again, Rose appears somewhat startled and perplexed after
reading the last line, but tries to compose herself)

Rose: These are beautiful. I see he quotes Catullus, and also
Virgil: "*Sunt lacrimae rerum et mentem mortalia tangunt.*" Did
Jack study Latin?

Millie: Yes, he went to the Catholic school here. The Dominican
Fathers teach them Latin from the fourth grade up. Jack did well in
school, but he stopped going after his parents and siblings died
during the flu epidemic in 1909...That quote says something about
tears and dying, doesn't it?

Rose: Yes, it says that mortal things touch the human heart, and
they bring tears…Yes… mortal hearts are touched by mortal
things. (Rose starts crying, then Millie too)

Millie: And immortal hearts are touched even more… You know,
it seems as if Jack had some kind of premonition about his death.

Rose (nervously): I see that they were all written around the same
time, from Sept. to Dec. 1910.

Millie: That was right before he left. He said a few times that he wanted to go to California, and even to Europe. We all thought he was dreaming. But then he left the day after Christmas that year. He didn't say anything about it before going, but he left a note. We still have it. (She gets note from bedroom)

"Dearest Family,
I thought it best to save you the trouble of trying to change my mind about heading out on my great world tour. I will be sure to write now and then to let you know how I'm doing. I don't think I should have too much trouble keeping housed and fed, what with all the poker skills I've picked up, and I can always draw if by chance I lose a game or two. Who knows, I may even get an occasional job to help keep me on my toes! You'll likely see me before too long with the girl of my dreams on my arm - since I know by now that she isn't in Chippawa Falls!
                                        I love you all,
                                               Jack

Rose: He sounds like quite a character! I regret not knowing him longer.

(Rose asks about the girl or girls referred to in the poems, but no one remembers him ever falling in love with any girl.)

Jeremy: But he sometimes spoke about meeting the woman of his dreams, that he would sail away with her on some boat (laughs)… He even called it his "Ship of Dreams". (Rose looks somewhat startled. Flashback of daydream of her and Jack on sailboat, then of newspaper clipping of Titanic as "Ship of Dreams".)

(Rose asks if she may read over the poems in her room. There she makes copies of them. Jack's Aunt Millie tell her that "The Song of the Silent Swan" is her favorite and that she knows it by heart.

Rose asks if Jack was very "religious", and learns that though he wasn't exactly "pious", he was very unselfish, helping others whenever he could, and went to Sunday Mass and monthly confession with the family, and prayed the rosary with them, although his religious fervor diminished and he stopped going to church after his family died, when he became withdrawn for several months, after which he spent much of his time in hunting and fishing, his art work, reading novels and poetry, and card playing. But Fr. Connolly took a special interest in him and helped Jack to become renewed in his faith, spending time with him, going fishing and hiking, and sharing a common interest in poetry and literature.)

(After several days with Jack's relatives, who persuade her to stay with them, Rose is introduced to his cousin Jeremy, returning home after a number of days away supervising a construction job. He bears a physical likeness to Jack, with a similar voice even. She is attracted to him. On Sunday morning Rose is invited to join the family in going to Mass. She declines graciously, partly at least because she thinks that Jeremy will be remaining at the house. As the family is exiting the front door...)

Mrs. Dawson: Let's go, Jeremy - you can fix your hair in the wagon!

(Rose suddenly changes her mind and joins them. At the consecration of the host at Mass, "...hic est enim Corpus meum"...)

Rose (whispering to Jeremy): Isn't that where "hocus pocus" comes from?

Jeremy (chuckling quietly): Well, a lot of non-Catholics think it's hocus pocus, but Catholics believe it's a miracle...Don't you believe in miracles?

Rose: I'm not sure…sometimes I'd like to.

(Rose learns that Jack and Jeremy were inseparable friends until the year before he left, when Jack became less interested in doing things together. Rose pries as much information as she can about Jack from Jeremy, including…)

Jeremy: Jack seemed to have a kind of sixth sense for things, especially when others needed help, like when uncle John, his father, got lost during a snowstorm, and once when I started getting cramps when I was swimming in the lake. He just seemed to know somehow when people were in danger and needed help….Rose, I hope you don't mind me asking, but did you.. um…like Jack in a… special way?

Rose (nervously): Well…I was *intrigued* by him, as you can imagine, him being so full of… life and all. But we hardly even knew each other.

(Rose and Jeremy do things together and soon fall in love. One day at Mass she hears the scripture reading: "Deep waters cannot quench love, neither can floods drown it." (Song of Songs 8:7) Rose asks the priest, Fr. Connolly after Mass where the passage is from, he tells her, and says some kind words to her.)

Rose: Father, did you know Jack very well?

Fr. Connolly: I knew him since he was a baby. A bright young lad and full of mischief (chuckles), but good, a big heart, and almost always cheerful. Cheerfulness is a good sign of life in the soul, and Jack… he had a lot of life. You could say he was like the sea in which his mortal remains now lie: he was deep, but not lacking a little foam and turbulence on top (smiles). We all miss him…But I feel confident that the sacrifice of his life has gained him a reward in the next. Dying for another is the supreme expression of love, and as the scriptures tell us, "love covers a multitude of sins." I'll always remember Jack's self-forgetfulness in helping and serving others. He was also a deep thinker, especially for someone so young. Have you seen some of his poetry?

Rose (crying): Yes. Oh Father, I miss him so much. More every day, the more I hear about him and think about him and read his poems and… I'm so confused, Father. I'm in love with Jeremy but I don't know if it's just that I see part of Jack in him or if I love him for himself….Sometimes I wish I had just died in the water with Jack.

Fr. C: Now, now, my child… You survived for a reason, Rose, and it is very possible, probable, in fact, that you love Jeremy both for himself as well as for what you see in him that reminds you of Jack. Jeremy is a good man and I believe he will make a very good husband and father. I can see the hand of divine providence in you and Jeremy meeting one another and falling in love after what you experienced with Jack. I would consider Jeremy as a gift from God… and even as a gift from Jack. You make a beautiful couple. I believe you will be happy together. The Greek philosopher Epictetus said that "he is a wise man who does not grieve for the thing which he has not, but rejoices for those which he has." Now don't worry. Trust in God. He has brought you this far. He will take you the rest of the way.

Rose: He'll certainly have to, because I know I can't do it on my own. I wasn't raised with as many *moral* demands as those of social etiquette. I think I may be getting in over my head, Father, especially marrying a Catholic.

Fr. C: That's just the point: we get in over our heads and then God gives us the strength to stay afloat. At times we can feel overwhelmed by the demands of living a life according to the

Gospel, but if we pray and trust in God rather than ourselves, He gives us the grace to persevere. But right at the beginning it can seem quite a daunting task…Have you ever read the *Confessions* of St. Augustine?

Rose: I tried to once several years ago, but I only got through a few chapters. When my mother saw me with the book she took it away and said it was a bunch of papist lies. It was in our Harvard Classics series, but she never noticed it until I started reading it. I didn't give it much thought after that.

Fr. C: Well, I highly recommend it. At the beginning of Augustine's conversion from his worldly and sensual life, he begins to feel quite certain in his heart that following Christ is what he has to do to find peace of soul and also salvation. But after so many years of living immorally he sees that the demands are too much for him, so he gets down on his knees and prays, "O Lord, do thou make me chaste…but not yet!" (Rose laughs.)

Rose: That sounds like a prayer right out of *my* book! (Both smile.)

Fr. C: There is also a poem that I think you would like, which I believe was also Jack's favorite. Have you heard of "The Hound of Heaven" by Francis Thompson?

Rose: No, I haven't, but I'd like to see it.

Fr. C: Here, you may borrow this book, which has it. It's about a soul, Thompson's in fact, trying to run from God, seeking various substitutes for Him, and God gently but relentlessly pursuing him. Knowing that Jack liked poetry, I showed it to him one day, and it wasn't long before he knew the entire poem from memory. He told me that it greatly helped him after the loss of his family led him to feelings of anger against God and then loss of faith.

Rose: Thank you very much, Father…for everything.

(Rose reads passages from the poem at home aloud during several scenes. Show verses while she reads them.)

The Hound of Heaven
I fled Him, down the nights and down the days;
I fled Him, down the arches of the years;
I fled Him, down the labyrinthine ways
Of my own mind; and in the mist of tears
I hid from Him, and under running laughter.
Up vistaed hopes I sped;
And shot, precipitated,
Adown Titanic glooms of chasmèd fears,
From those strong Feet that followed, followed after.
But with unhurrying chase,
And unperturbèd pace,
Deliberate speed, majestic instancy,
They beat - and a voice beat
More instant than the Feet -
"All things betray thee, who betrayest Me."

I pleaded, outlaw-wise,
By many a hearted casement, curtained red,
Trellised with intertwining charities;
(For, though I knew His love Who followèd,
Yet was I sore adread
Lest, having Him, I must have naught beside.)
But, if one little casement parted wide,
The gust of his approach would clash it to.
Fear wist not to evade, as Love wist to pursue.
Across the margent of the world I fled,
And troubled the gold gateways of the stars,

Smiting for shelter on their clangèd bars;
Fretted to dulcet jars
And silvern chatter the pale ports o' the moon.
I said to dawn, Be sudden - to eve, Be soon;
With thy young skiey blossoms heap me over
From this tremendous Lover -
Float thy vague veil about me, lest He see!
I tempted all His servitors, but to find
My own betrayal in their constancy,
In faith to Him their fickleness to me,
Their traitorous trueness, and their loyal deceit.
To all swift things for swiftness did I sue;
Clung to the whistling mane of every wind....

Fear wist not to evade as Love wist to pursue.
Still with unhurrying chase,
And unperturbèd pace,
Deliberate speed, majestic instancy,
Came on the following Feet,
And a Voice above their beat -
"Naught shelters thee, who wilt not shelter Me." ....

I laughed in the morning's eyes.
I triumphed and I saddened with all weather,
Heaven and I wept together,
And its sweet tears were salt with mortal mine;
Against the red throb of its sunset-heart
I laid my own to beat,
And share commingling heat;
But not by that, by that, was eased my human smart.
In vain my tears were wet on Heaven's grey cheek.
For ah ! we know not what each other says,
These things and I ; in sound *I* speak -
Their sound is but their stir, they speak by silences.
Nature, poor stepdame, cannot slake my drouth;

Let her, if she would owe me,
Drop yon blue bosom-veil of sky, and show me
The breasts o' her tenderness;
Never did any milk of hers once bless
My thirsting mouth.
Nigh and nigh draws the chase,
With unperturbèd pace,
Deliberate speed, majestic instancy;
And past those noisèd Feet
A Voice comes yet more fleet -
"Lo! naught contents thee, who content'st not Me."

Naked I wait thy Love's uplifted stroke!
My harness piece by piece Thou hast hewn from me,
And smitten me to my knee;
I am defenseless utterly.
I slept, methinks, and woke,
And, slowly gazing, find me stripped in sleep.
In the rash lustihead of my young powers,
I shook the pillaring hours
And pulled my life upon me; grimed with smears,
I stand amid the dust o' the mounded years -
My mangled youth lies dead beneath the heap.
My days have crackled and gone up in smoke,
Have puffed and burst as sun-starts on a stream....

Ah! is Thy love indeed
A weed, albeit an amaranthine weed,
Suffering no flowers except its own to mount?
Ah! must -
Designer infinite! -
Ah! must Thou char the wood ere Thou canst limn with it?....

Such is; what is to be?
The pulp so bitter, how shall taste the rind?....

His name I know, and what his trumpet saith.
Whether man's heart or life it be which yields
Thee harvest, must Thy harvest-fields
Be dunged with rotten death?
Now of that long pursuit
Comes on at hand the bruit;
That Voice is round me like a bursting sea:
"And is thy earth so marred,
Shattered in shard on shard?
Lo, all things fly thee, for thou fliest me!
"Strange, piteous, futile thing!
Wherefore should any set thee love apart?
Seeing none but I makes much of naught" (He said),
"And human love needs human meriting,
How hast thou merited -
Of all man's clotted clay the dingiest clot?
Alack, thou knowest not
How little worthy of any love thou art!
Whom wilt thou find to love ignoble thee,
Save Me, save only Me?
All which I took from thee I did but take,
Not for thy harms,
But just that thou might'st seek it in My arms.
All which thy child's mistake
Fancies as lost, I have stored for thee at home;
Rise, clasp My hand, and come!"
Halts by me that footfall;
Is my gloom, after all,
Shade of His hand, outstretched caressingly?
"Ah, fondest, blindest, weakest,
I am He Whom thou seekest!
Thou dravest love from thee, who dravest me."

Francis Thompson (1859-1907)

(Rose then looks up the scripture passage, "Deep waters cannot quench love..." at home, and again imagines Jack sinking into the deep. She then sees that the passage that immediately follows says, "Were a man to offer all the wealth of his house to buy love, contempt is all he would purchase.") (Flashback of Caledon giving necklace to Rose)

Rose (visiting Fr. Connolly again): Thank you so much, Father, for sharing "The Hound of Heaven" with me. I can't remember ever reading a more powerful, yet so beautiful a poem. And knowing that Jack liked it so much has made it even more special for me. I feel closer to him when I read it... Oh, Father, if Jeremy asks me to marry him, I don't think I could live with myself if I didn't tell him about me and Jack.

Fr. C: Yes, that would be wise, at least that you loved each other. But you need not tell him everything, that the two of you had intimate relations. That would be unnecessary, and could cause more problems than it would prevent. Being honest with someone we love does not mean telling them everything about our past. Prudence dictates that some things should remain between us and God, as well as with our spiritual director, someone with whom we can entrust our conscience.

(Rose also tells him that she cannot forgive the Titanic survivors who refused to help save Jack and the others perishing in the water. Fr. C is the only one except for Molly that Rose tells about having intimate relations with Jack.)

Fr. Connolly: God is less offended by our sins of weakness, as when we succumb to the temptations of the flesh, than by the sins we hold in our heart, such as pride, envy, and refusing to love others. If we truly love others we should be willing to forgive them. To forgive and to seek forgiveness: on this hinges so much in our spiritual lives, our relationship with other people, and our relationship with God. Pray that you may receive this grace. I will be praying for you too.

(Jeremy proposes to Rose)

Rose: Jeremy, there is something I have to tell you before I answer. It's that I didn't tell you everything before about my feelings for Jack. But I can't keep it from you now. I fell in love with Jack. I left my fiance for him. I would have married Jack if he had survived. I didn't think it was right that I tell you before... Would you still want to marry me after knowing that?

Jeremy: Yes. I love you, Rose. And I want to marry you. (Smiling) ... even though that rascal cousin of mine found you first and got you to fall in love with him!

Rose: Oh Jeremy, I love you too... and I would be honored and happy to be your wife! (They kiss.)

Jeremy (later, talking to his mother): You know, I could see by her intense interest in anything about Jack that there was something going on between them. But at least she was honest enough to tell me. That's a good sign, I think.

Millie: I would say so too. I like Rose very much, and would be very happy to have her as my daughter-in-law.

"At that time it was very unusual for one, especially a woman, to marry into a Catholic family without becoming a Catholic. I was not planning on doing it at the time, but for some reason that is difficult to explain, the more time I spent with Jeremy and his family, and also their friends, as well as with Fr. Connolly, the more I just wanted to be like them... But possibly even more so, I wanted to be like Jack."

(Rose becomes a Catholic, the couple get married. Before the end of the wedding Rose takes a bouquet of flowers and places it before the statue of Our Lady Star of the Sea, then kneels before it and prays for a moment.)

(Molly comes out for the wedding. During the reception, alone with Rose…)

Molly: I'm so happy for you, Rose. You look absolutely stunning. More beautiful than I've ever seen you. It's too bad your mother couldn't be here to see you now.

Rose: You know my mother. She *wouldn't* be here, even if she were invited. She wouldn't be caught dead among such unsophisticated Catholics, much less with Jack's relatives.

Molly: Yes, I suppose you're right. Even I wouldn't have ever expected in a thousand years that you would turn papist! I could have just as easily imagined you becoming a Hindu snake charmer! (They both laugh.) But I guess it's like they say, When in Rome, do as the papists - I mean, Romans - do. (They laugh)

Rose: To tell you the truth, Molly, at first I found the whole Catholic atmosphere a little frightening, but I gradually got accustomed to it. Being around such loving people as the Dawsons has made the transition so much easier. And you must meet Fr. Connolly. He has helped me more than I can say. And he's so wise, and quite witty as well. I think a few minutes with him might go a long way in dissolving into thin air some of the notions you were raised with about Catholics.

 Molly: I'll have you know, young lady, that some of my very closest…*acquaintances* are
Catholics. (They laugh.)

Rose: Oh, here comes Father now…Father, this is Molly Brown, about whom I've told you so much. Molly, this is Fr. Connolly. I wouldn't be here right now if it weren't for him.

Molly: Well, that much I can believe! (They all laugh.)

Rose: I hope you will both excuse me. Jeremy seems to be calling for me.

(Show Molly and Fr. C talking and laughing)

"As I expected, Fr. C and Molly hit it off wonderfully. They must have spent at least an hour together during the reception."

Fr. C: …and so Napoleon's blood is just boiling at this point, and he shouts at Cardinal Consalvi, "You tell the Pope that if he doesn't sign this agreement I will *destroy* the Church!" And Consalvi calmly replies to him, "Your sovereignty, with all due respect, if popes, cardinals, bishops and priests over the last eighteen hundred years have not been able to destroy the Church, it is difficult to believe that that *you* will be able to." (Molly laughs)

Molly (a little later, along with several other ladies): Isn't it hard to deny that the Church has vigorously opposed much of the scientific and social progress that has taken place in modern times? Some even say that the Church would bring us back to the Dark Ages.

Fr. C: It's rather funny that anyone could think *that*, since it was primarily the Church that brought Western Civilization *out of* the Dark Ages, especially through the institution of Benedictine monasticism. It was the monks who preserved the knowledge of literature, law, engineering, agriculture and the rest of the patrimony of the Greco-Roman world during those chaotic times when the various barbarian hoards were overrunning Europe and destroying practically everything in their path. Christianity, so far from belonging to the Dark Ages, was the one path across the Dark Ages that was *not* dark. It was a shining bridge connecting two shining civilizations - the Roman and the high Middle Ages. The most absurd thing that could be said of the Church is the thing we have all heard said of it. How can we say that the Church wishes to bring us back into the Dark Ages when it was the only thing that ever brought us *out* of them? As for progress, the Church has never opposed progress as such, only what degrades the human person and violates the dignity of man, oftentimes in the *name* of progress. For two hundred years now political and cultural leaders have been doing everything they can to liberate Western society from the influence of religion, especially Christianity. But deep down they mostly want to liberate *themselves* from the moral order, of which Christianity, and especially the Church is to them an unpleasant reminder. Such people talk about "freedom" when they are actually proposing a form of bondage, slavery to base instincts and passions and selfish appetites, which is all that remains when the objective moral order is discarded. Seeking liberation from the Church and the moral law is actually seeking liberation from reason, which these people think they are exalting. And since reason is what makes a man a human being, or in other words a free moral agent, all this talk about "enlightenment" and the exaltation of reason and progress can be very misleading. Only when our reason is subject to the divine law will our passions be subject to reason. There will always be progress in theoretical and applied science, or technology, but there can never be any true *social* progress outside the moral order, which we do not decide for ourselves or by consensus, but which is intrinsic to our human nature and derives ultimately from God. This objective moral order the Church has always and will always continue to uphold and proclaim.

Molly: Well, Father, I think I'll have to put my reason to work on that, but it may just take me a few years. (The other ladies laugh)

Fr. C (smiling): Well, let me give you an image to illustrate my point. Think of our lower passions as a horse and our reason as a rider, first breaking in and taming the horse until he is able to direct the horse where he wants it to go, and spurring it on or reining it in as he so chooses. Now if you have the case of a horse galloping off toward a cliff with a blindfolded man on its back, it is only in some analogous sense of the term that one can say that the man is really *riding* the horse. Now if the man represents reason, the blindfold represents reason rejecting any guidance from anything outside of itself, and therefore rendering itself blind to the deepest and most fundamental truths about life, about our origin and destiny, and the ultimate meaning of human existence.

Molly: Well, now that's a little easier to follow, don't you agree, ladies? (They all agree.) Now I won't need a few years to mentally digest what you're saying, Father… Maybe just a few *months*. (The ladies all laugh, Fr. C smiles.)

"Molly ended up staying in Chippewa Falls an extra three days than planned, and I'm fairly sure it was not just because of me." (Show Molly And Fr. C going for a walk.)

(Rose soon finds that though she loves Jeremy, she finds it difficult to give her whole heart to him, he is too different from Jack in personality and it was seeing Jack in him that first drew her to him, and then afterwards knowing that the two were so close for many years. Rose bears this new burden stoically, finding what little consolation she can in bonding with her new relations, especially her mother-in-law Millie, and in thinking about Jack. She also often recites his poems from memory when alone. At times she imagines Jack's face replacing Jeremy's when he makes love to her. She confesses this and also seeks guidance and consolation from Fr. C.)

Rose: Father, in some of what I've heard that Jack said and in what he wrote, it almost seems like he could see into the future. He talked about sailing away on his "ship of dreams", which as you know was what some people called the Titanic, and he wrote about falling in love with his "sweet Rose", although no one recalls any girl he may have loved. And it even seems he might have had a premonition of his own impending death. Sometimes it's scary to think about it all. Plus I dream about him, and they're not like regular dreams. They seem more like real life, and I always remember them.

Fr. C.: Well, sometimes it does happen that one can see events that will take place in the future, but it is a rare occurrence. But then again, "ship of dreams" and "sweetest Rose" may be merely coincidences, and it may just have been that he reflected deeply on the mystery of life and death. We all should… As for the dreams, it's understandable that such an overpowering experience combining both love and extreme trauma would make them more intense and more frequent than other dreams. It's always safer to look for natural causes for things first. There are indeed preternatural and supernatural realms, but we shouldn't seek them as explanations for phenomena until all natural explanations are exhausted. Remember "Occam's Razor"?

Rose: Yes: *Non sunt multiplicanda entia sine necessitate.*

Fr. C: That's right. And that includes the reasons and causes of things. We shouldn't multiply them without necessity. (Rose nods) …You know, Jack once gave me a poem. It's on the lighter side. Let me show it to you…(He gets it.)

(Rose reads it aloud)

I sometimes find it hard to tell
If I am on the road to hell. ("Oh!")

One day I went to see a priest;
He said I was a filthy beast, (she laughs)
And that I'd surely go to hell
Unless I started tithing well.
And then I saw a minister,
Who looked to me quite sinister;
He said, "You Catholics are all jerks, (shakes her head, smiling, for
the rest of it)
Believe like us and you'll be saved -
But as a Papist you're depraved!"
So then I saw a rabbi Jew,
Who said, "In hell there's only few -
And most of them are priests and Arabs,
Folks like us – we'll be like cherubs -
But Israel we must support
To be the chosen, righteous sort."
So then I went to a psychiatrist;
"There is no sin!" he said, quite pissed;
"It's all a myth, all superstition,
Giving priests more ammunition!
Just give in to all your passions,
Give up all your Puritan fashions -
And first of all you need more sex,
To overcome your God complex!"
Dismayed, I went to my friend Mike.
He said, "Man, don't believe that Kike,
That bigot, or that stupid priest,
Or that deranged and godless psych!
Believe me when I say, my friend,
That God is good and would not send
A soul to hell who sought to love
His neighbor and the Lord above."
I felt relieved… until at least
He said, "Now see a different priest." (laughs)
I never saw a different priest,

And all my fears have just increased.
So still I find it hard to tell
If I am on the road to hell.
Oh, well.... (laughs)

Rose: It seems as if there were many sides to Jack Dawson.

Fr. C: Yes, there were… he was certainly one of a kind.

(At Mass, during the words of the Our Father: "…*dimitte nobis debita nostra, sicut et nos dimittimus debitoribus nostris*" Rose shows painful concentration in her expression; also when praying it together with the Dawson family, in English.)

(Rose tells Mrs. Dawson how she had grown further and further away from her mother. Millie consoles her.)

Millie: We always have a loving Mother in heaven to whom we can turn in all our pains and trials and difficulties of life. (Rose glances at their statue of Mary.) That's Our Lady of Lourdes. Fr. Connolly brought it back from France for us.

Rose: I've heard people talk about miracles of healing there.

Millie: Yes, Lourdes is where Mary appeared to a young girl and where many people are miraculously cured when they enter the waters of the spring there. I hear they even have doctors and scientists there to verify the cures.

Rose: Hmm…that's quite amazing.

"I was wondering at the time if that includes the curing of broken hearts."

"Three months after our wedding, I came to find out that the long arm of Caledon Hockley could reach all the way to Chippewa Falls. When Molly told me in NY that Caledon knew that I had survived and that I had taken Jack's name as my own, I felt pretty certain that I had not yet completely escaped from him. I knew he had a vindictive nature, and the insult and humiliation he must have felt on account of my rejecting him for Jack must have burned deep within him… One thing he would often say was that he always won. But for him winning sometimes meant seeing to it that his adversaries or his competition suffered. In my case he chose to target the person closest to me, my husband. Jeremy often liked to have a few beers with some of his friends and co-workers on Saturday evenings. I would have preferred that he be with me, but it was just one of the things that the men did. One Saturday two of Caledon's men entered the tavern and sat down. After a little while, one of them came up to Jeremy."

"Excuse me, are you Jeremy Dawson?"
"Yes I am."
"So you must be the husband of Rose Dawson, who survived the sinking of the Titanic."
"That's true."
"I've heard some amazing things about how she was saved by Jack Dawson… your cousin, I believe."
"Yes, Jack died while trying to save Rose."
"Hmm…I also heard that he might have saved her from, uh… something a little more… say, maybe, um…carnal frustration?"

Jeremy (standing up): What the hell are you talking about, and who the hell do you think you are coming in here and saying that kind of shit?! If you're looking for trouble, buddy, then you've found it!

Man: No, no - Sorry, I'm not looking for trouble, just trying to get to the bottom of a little… mystery that a lot of people are trying to solve. No offense intended, I assure you. (He finishes his drink, tips his hat, then goes outside with his partner.)

Jeremy: Mystery! What the hell is this? I should just kick his ass right now! (Starts walking toward door)

Friend: Wait a second, Jeremy. These guys look like they were sent here for something. Let's look and see where they're going, and then maybe find out what's going on here.

(They get up and watch the two men get into a car and drive off.)

Jeremy: If they're working for somebody, I'm going to find out who, and why. I'm not going to take this bullshit!

"Jeremy never came home that night. They found him the next day at his construction site, having been killed apparently from a fall. One of Jeremy's friends later told me about the two men in the tavern, and how one of them had said something that offended Jeremy, but he didn't say what it was… On the same day that I heard about Jeremy I also heard about how two men had crashed into a tree in their automobile and had both died. I found out it was the same two men. That night I felt very troubled and could not sleep until about 3:00 a.m. After I finally was able to sleep I had a dream about two men driving in a car (Show men joking and laughing, then suddenly noticing Jack standing in their path, then swerving to avoid him and slamming into a tree, both going through windshield and dying in agony). It was very disturbing. Then I only saw Jack."

Jack: I am still with you, Rose. I will always be with you.

Rose: Oh Jack!…What about Jeremy?

Jack: It was Jeremy's time. Just as it was my time to go when you and I were in the water together. It's all part of a bigger picture, one that you can't perceive yet because it's too big for mortal eyes to see, and too simple for the mind to grasp. But don't be afraid. You will know soon what to do. I'll be with you, Rose.

"Then I woke up. As always when I dreamed of Jack, I woke up feeling peaceful and untroubled. And I always remembered the dreams.

(Show several women talking and glancing over at Rose outside the Dawson house.) "Even before the funeral I noticed that some people were talking in hushed tones about something and looking at me with furtive looks. I soon found out it wasn't all about Jeremy's death, or about his drinking. It was also about the rumors which the men in the tavern had started. It was Millie who told me about the rumors."

(Show Jeremy's funeral...)

Fr. Connolly (giving homily): My heart and my prayers go out to Rose, Millie, and to all of the family at this painful and difficult time.

I would like to share some thoughts on Jeremy's life and his death, especially in the context of God's Providence and his plan for our lives, that is to say, the "big picture," one that, since it *is* so big, we often find it very difficult to see.

It as been said that there are two things that a person cannot look at steadily: one is the sun, and the other is death. We can only glance briefly at the sun because it is too bright, we can't look at it even though it is by the light of the sun that everything else becomes visible. We see the things of this world by the light of that which we are unable to look at, although we know it's there. It is difficult to look at death because it is too painfully *dark* for us to look at, a fearful and painfully dark mystery, especially the death of a loved one, or when it involves the thought of our own approaching death. Love seems to contradict death. To say to a person, "I love you" means: I don't want to accept your death; I *protest* against your dying and being taken from me. The thought of death forces us, or at least calls us, to look more seriously at our own lives, at our own mortality, and at the ultimate meaning of our existence.

Every one of us has been affected in some way by Jeremy's life and by his death. His death grieves us very much, some of us tremendously. Those of us, however, who believe in an all-knowing, all-loving and all-powerful God, and even more so those who believe that the key to the mystery of death is found in the person of Jesus Christ, as well as the key to the mystery of life and of suffering and of moral evil—those of us who believe, who have received this gift of faith will find, along with the sorrow that we experience, also some strength, hope, consolation, and confidence that almighty God can and indeed does bring good out of evil. Even on a natural and human level we can often see something similar. We know that hardships, personal trials and suffering often lead to greater strength or great accomplishments, or greater knowledge and understanding, or growth in virtue, or greater love.

But it is on the supernatural level that we see the greatest example of good coming out of evil. We see it in the life of Christ, in the torture and crucifixion of the Son of God who came into this world —the greatest evil ever committed -   from which came the greatest good—salvation—the victory over death, and over sin, which is the ultimate cause of death. Christ showed us by his glorious resurrection from the dead that death does *not* have the last say in our lives, because he conquered death for us by freely choosing to suffer and die for us, the innocent victim paying the debt for our sins and then rising from the dead in order to share with us his eternal life and happiness in heaven.

In the beautiful and moving gospel account of the resurrection of

Lazarus from the dead (John 11), Martha and Mary, the sisters of Lazarus, both address Jesus with the words, "Lord, if you had been here, my brother would not have died." And Martha adds, "Yet even now I know that whatever you ask from God, God will give you." Jesus said to her, "I am the resurrection and the life; he who believes in me, though he die, shall live, and whoever lives and believes in me will never die."

Many people, however, live and die without much clue to the true meaning and purpose of life. There is a true story about a man who, when asked what he would like written on his tomb, said: "You shall write the words, 'Here lies a fool, who went out of this world without knowing how he entered it'." It is unfortunate that many people, like him, do not know that the ultimate purpose of our life here on earth is to strive to love God above all things, and to love and serve one another, and by doing so, or at least repenting of not having done so, to save our souls, to ultimately be with God forever in heaven. God's revealed truth teaches us that this life is only a preparation and a proving ground, so to speak, for something unimaginably greater. St Paul tells us that "no eye has seen, no ear has heard, nor has it so much as entered the mind of man, what God has prepared for those who love him" (1 Cor 2:9). "For this slight momentary affliction is preparing us for an eternal weight of glory beyond all comparison" (2 Cor 4:17)." In fact, "our sufferings in this present life," he says, "are as nothing compared with the glory to be revealed in us" in heaven (Rom 8:18). St Paul also writes: "O death, where is your victory? O death, where is your sting? The sting of death is sin…but thanks be to God, who gives us the victory through our Lord Jesus Christ" (1 Cor 15:55-57). So for those with faith, death, though it does bring sorrow, has indeed lost its sting, there *is* victory over death. For them death has become like a stingless bee, since its stinger has lodged itself in the body of Christ on the Cross.

Science tells us that every poisonous plant contains its own antidote. So it is with death. Death is now the condition for entry into eternal life. As St Paul writes to Timothy: "If we have died with [Christ] we shall also live with him; if we hold out to the end we shall also reign with him."

It has been said that our life on earth "is a moment out of eternity to say Yes or No to divine love." I believe that Jeremy said Yes to that divine love.

I also believe that one of the reasons God took Jeremy when he did was because God knew that his soul *was* ready.

In the Book of Wisdom we read: "The just man, though he die early, will be at rest.... For he was pleasing to God and was loved by him, and while living among sinners was taken up. He was snatched away lest evil despoil his mind or deceit beguile his soul....for his soul was pleasing to the Lord, therefore he took him quickly from the midst of wickedness. Yet the peoples saw and did not understand, nor did they take this into account...." (Wis 4: 7, 10-11, 13-14).

Though our faith and trust in God's mercy should give us confidence, that doesn't mean we shouldn't continue to pray for the repose of Jeremy's soul. He may very well need our prayers to help him take that final step into the glory of heaven. In the Bible we read that it is a holy and upright thing to pray for the dead and offer sacrifices for them, so that they may be released from the purification required for their sins (2 Macc 12:44-46; cf. Lk 12:59). And especially offering for them the holy sacrifice of the Mass.

Another reason why God permitted Jeremy to die at this time, I believe, is so that many of us would also be inspired to say Yes to his love, and for those who already do say Yes, to grow in that love. Someone once said that a funeral is an occasion for those attending to come to terms with *what is*, that is, with reality. In other words, most of the time we're tempted to imagine that our own death is way afar off and we need not bother thinking about it, nor of God's judgment of our souls when we die. To be confronted with death is to be reminded that we too can at any moment be snatched away and suddenly appear before the throne of God. And this has a way of concentrating our minds more than most life experiences. It makes us realize that we're really not in control. It tends to make us rearrange our priorities, to think about whether we are placing too much importance on things that won't really matter when we die or are harmful to our souls, and whether we are placing too little importance on the things that will matter a lot, like pure and unselfish love, and the pressing need to be deeply converted to God *today*; so that when, as Jesus said, the unexpected "thief" comes in the night, that is to say, death, we will be clothed with the armor of God's grace rather than veiled in the darkness of sin.

In grieving for a loved one we tend to be more open to what the spiritual writers call "the great thought," the *magna cogitatio,* that is, the thought of *eternity*. Eternity is called the "great thought" because eternity is the great and all-important reality, compared to which this brief life is not even the blink of an eye, and it is a reality that every one of us will enter, and usually sooner than we expect. Each one of us has a soul to save, and an eternity that awaits us.

But to say Yes to God can at times be very difficult. In times of affliction such as the loss of a loved one, especially one like Jeremy taken so suddenly in the prime of his life, we may not only feel great sorrow, but also confusion, or even resentment or anger.

It may tempt us to feel anger or resentment toward God or to lose our faith in him, as if he had betrayed us. But God can't betray us. We can only betray him. But we don't have to *understand* what he is doing to believe that he *is* infinitely good and that he loves us.

Through the prophet Isaiah God says: "My thoughts are not your thoughts, neither are your ways my ways. For as the heavens are higher than the earth, so are my ways higher than your ways, and my thoughts than your thoughts" (Isaiah 55:8-9). We definitely need God. He made us. We belong to him. The only reason why our lives have any meaning and value at all is that they are a gift from God. Even the power we have to rebel against God or to deny him comes from him. If there is no God, then there is no such thing as right and wrong, all moral discourse is meaningless, and so is love. All that remains is the selfish pursuit of pleasure and the will to power. And that's unfortunately what we see a lot of in our world…. And if we look deeply within *ourselves*, we'll see the same thing. Its traditional name is sin. It's something we all share, ever since the Fall from grace of our first parents, Adam and Eve, which we call *Original* Sin, the effects of which, including death, remain with us even after Baptism removes the sin itself.

No, there is nothing wrong with God, there's only something wrong with us. Someone once asked the English writer G. K. Chesterton, What's wrong with the world? He said: "I am." There is much wisdom in that answer. Humility too—and truth. That mysterious world within us, however, is a world which, like the sun and like death, can be painfully difficult to look at, more difficult to look at than the outside world, but one which is also in need of spiritual healing from the Divine Physician.

So if we feel extreme sorrow at Jeremy's death, or if we feel confused or angry, or are even tempted to despair, then it may be a good time to go into our room and close the door, and talk to God in the secret of our heart—even if that means complaining to him. Because even complaining to God is talking to God, and talking to God is prayer, and prayer is the key to God's heart. And it unlocks our own as well—from the inside. Along with frequent and devout reception of the sacraments, it is prayer especially that keeps us not only on the way of salvation, but even on the way of sanity. And of inner peace. God says in the psalm: "Call to me in your distress. I will free you and you shall honor me" (Ps 50:15). In another psalm we read: "The salvation of the just comes from the Lord, their stronghold in times of distress. The Lord helps them and delivers them: for their refuge is in him" (Ps 37:39-40). And in another psalm: "The Lord is close to the brokenhearted; and those who are crushed in spirit he saves" (Ps 34:19). Many of us are brokenhearted. But if there is one good thing about a broken heart, it's that it is an *open* heart, one that is especially open to the promptings of God's grace. There is a novel in which one of the characters, a holy priest, says these profound words. He says: "One has to *accept* sorrow for it to be of any healing power....When you understand what *accepted* sorrow means, you will understand everything. It is the secret of life."

Though the death of our loved ones brings sorrow in its wake, for those who follow Christ there is no reason to fear our own death, as unbelievers do. In the letter to the Hebrews we read that Christ came to free "those who through fear of death had been slaves their whole life long." For the fear of death, like sin, which is its cause, is a type of slavery. And Christ frees us from both.

My opening words about the sun and death being both painful to look at are actually only partially true, because there *are* ways to more easily look at both of them. Just as one can look at the sun through a dark lens or through its reflection in the water, so also one can look upon death, especially the death of a loved one or our own approaching death, through the prism of the Cross of Christ. It was the Father's will that Christ suffer and die for our sins, and it is also his will that we trustingly accept what comes to us from his hands. For, as Dante wrote in what has been called the most beautiful line ever written in poetry, "E'n la sua volontate `e nostra pace" ("In His will is our peace.") (Paradiso, 3, 85)

Jeremy has preceded us into the next life. And we all shall very soon follow. In the meantime let us keep our torches lit, with the oil of faith, hope and love, as the seven wise virgins in the parable who were awake and ready when the Bridegroom arrived. To them, but not to the seven foolish ones who brought no oil, he opened the door to the wedding feast, meaning heaven, where those who have passed the test during their lifetime and have been found faithful to the Lord will enter into unimaginable happiness with him.

Each one of us should be grateful to God for bringing Jeremy into our lives, for allowing us to share in his love and his friendship and the many wonderful gifts God bestowed on him. And we should even try to make a heroic effort, with prayerful abandonment to God's will, of trustingly accepting the fact that God knows what he is about, that he sees what we don't see, that he sees the "big picture," and that he orders all things for our ultimate good, which is our salvation, even though sometimes, being the Divine Physician that he is, he gives us bitter tasting medicine, or even performs painful spiritual surgery on us. You may recall the words of Job in the Old Testament, who in his affliction says: "Naked I came from my mother's womb, and naked I shall return. The Lord hath given, and the Lord hath taken away. Blessed be the name of the Lord" (Job 1:21). That last part can be very hard to say when someone is painfully snatched away from our lives, but we can at least pray for the grace and for the strength to be able to say it. If we do so we can also trust that one day, God willing, we shall see Jeremy again in the Land of the Living, where every tear shall be wiped away and the sounds of weeping shall have given way to songs of rejoicing—forever.

I would like to close with a poem Jeremy's cousin Jack, who died on the Titanic, wrote after his parents and brother and sister died during the flu epidemic of 1909:

Temporary Parting
Rejoicing in the presence of the ones we love today,

We feel the pain of separation when they're gone tomorrow;
It makes us wonder if this life is just a tragic play,
If there is rhyme and reason in what fills us with such sorrow.
But if we look beyond this life upon which we are leaning
And trust that just as life's a gift, there's reason too in death,
We'll see the loving hand of Him Who gives all things their meaning,
Who in the glorious world beyond will give them back their breath.

(Show Rose writing in her diary)

"After the funeral, I told Millie about Jack and me being in love, but not about Caledon possibly having something to do with Jeremy's death as a way of getting back at me."

Millie: Jeremy told me about you and Jack being in love. I think it's beautiful that Jack lived long enough to find his "sweet rose", even if he was to see it and hold it for such a brief time. Now God has taken both of them from you, and from me, but only for a little while. As Father said, "The Lord hath given, and the Lord hath taken away. Blessed be the name of the Lord." We must trust in Him. His ways are not always our ways, but they are always for the best. That is what our faith tells us... And I want you to know that I will always consider you my daughter-in-law, Rose. Always. Even though Jeremy is gone, you are part of the family, and I love you. (They embrace.)

Rose: Oh, Millie, that means so much to me... But I want to confide something to you that only two other people know. Would you have accepted me if you knew that Jack and I had had relations together?

Millie: I don't see why I wouldn't. Rose, I am a sinner in need of God's mercy. Who am I to stand in judgment of someone else?

When you became a Catholic you made your peace with God. Or maybe even before. And Fr. Connolly told me that by giving up his own life to save yours, Jack made the supreme sacrifice and would be rewarded for it, despite any sins he may not have had time to confess. Come here, my daughter.

Rose (crying): Oh Mother! I'm so sorry! (They embrace)

"Despite my growing attachment to Millie, after the funeral I knew I had to leave Chippewa Falls, and I also resolved never again to speak about ever having been on the Titanic to anyone, with the exception of several priests I trusted, to whom I told everything, knowing that what I told them would never be repeated. Before I left, however, I received a telegram. It did not say from whom it was sent, but I knew who it was. It just said, "Condolences on your loss. Better luck next time." No one could have written that but Caledon…. Although the Dawsons insisted that I stay, I knew I couldn't. I went to Milwaukee with the intention, not without some uncertainty, of continuing on to New York after a few days. Molly was looking forward to my coming. But once in Milwaukee I met some wonderful people and soon found work as a clothes designer…. I also taught ballet… I wrote to Molly telling her of my decision not to come. She was disappointed, but she also knew that being closer to Caledon and around people he knew in New York would put me in greater danger…. After a few months I met Darrell Calvert. Although I wanted to keep to myself my having been on the Titanic, I didn't want to tell him anything untrue. I told him that I came over by ship with my mother, that I had heard how beautiful Wisconsin was, so after visiting California I went there on my way back to New York, but met Jeremy, married, then lost him in what appeared to be an accident. Darrell and I got married and had five children together. (Show scenes of home life) I became a full-time mom although I continued to design clothing periodically. The ballet lessons were limited to my two daughters and a few of their friends….Molly would come out and visit almost every year. The children called her aunt Molly and they loved her as much as she loved them

Child 1: Aunt Molly, tell us stories about the Titanic!

Child 2: Yeah! Tell us stories about the Titanic!

Rose: Children, you know that it was a very traumatic experience for Aunt Molly. It's not polite to always ask her about it.

Molly: It's alright. If I'm going to talk about it to anyone, then you children certainly ought to be included. (She glances at Rose.) Now you kids just never get enough of that ship!... Well, did I ever tell you about how I came upon a young lady and a young man who were having a spitting contest at the stern of the ship?

Child 1: No! Tell us about it!

Child 2: Yeah! Tell us about it!

(Rose shakes her head and rolls her eyes, though smiling)

Molly: Well, I was walking along the deck with several ladies, one of whom was the mother of this young lady. All of us were in first class, of course. But the young man was from steerage, or third class. So when we got the couple's attention they were startled and embarrassed, as you can imagine, the girl's mother witnessing this spectacle of social impropriety and all. And the young man doesn't realize it, but he has spittle on his chin (they laugh), and so I try to subtly signal him by pointing to my own chin, so he finally wipes it off. But you should have seen the expression on the other ladies' faces, especially the girl's mother! She looked at that young lad as if he were the devil himself! (laughter)

"Molly continued to be a great support for me and my one friend to whom I could always turn. She was also the only connection I still had to the world that I left behind…I continued to think of Jack, especially when I was alone. They were bitter-sweet thoughts, giving me both comfort and sorrow…. I also memorized his poems, and they became, along with the diamond, a tangible sign of the bond we made and which I dreamed would continue for the rest of my life, and then into eternity. These thoughts would at times lead to pangs of guilt. It was as if I was living a double life, one with Darrell and the children, and another with Jack. And then sometimes I would wonder, What if I had returned to New York? What if I had done this or done that? It made me sometimes doubt if the life I had now was the one I should have chosen."

Rose (in confession): …Father, it's not just that I still hold on to Jack or that I can't forgive the people who caused him to die, it's… everything. My life has completely changed. In so many ways it's better, but it seems like I've lost so much of my…freedom. I'm at other people's beck and call continuously. And it seems like most of my time is just spent cleaning up after other people's messes. I don't think I'll ever make a very good Catholic, Father.

Fr. Padolano: Well, believe it or not, that's a pretty good attitude to have. It shows humility. The Lord will never abandon the humble of heart. I'd be much more concerned if you thought you were a *good* Catholic, because that would most likely stem from the sin of pride, which prevents true self-knowledge, and the conversion of heart which we all need. And if it is any comfort to you in being a loving wife and mother, especially when you're "cleaning up after others' messes," think about how God Himself is continually cleaning up after *our* messes, the messes we make in our own lives. For this we should be thankful…. For your penance, try to meditate for five minutes or more on the words of our Lord: 'forgive us our trespasses as we forgive those who trespass against us', calling to mind that God will be merciful to us to the extent that we in turn are also willing to forgive. I imagine you remember your Shakespeare: 'The quality of mercy is not strain'd,/ It droppeth as the gentle rain from heaven/ Upon the place beneath: it is twice blest;/ It blesseth him that gives and him that takes…/ And earthly power doth then show likest God's/ When mercy seasons justice…./ Though justice be thy plea, consider this,/ That, in the course of justice, none of us/ Should see salvation: we do pray for mercy;/ And that same prayer doth teach us all to render/ The deeds of mercy'. (Merchant of Venice, 4, 1, 184) We also see in the book of Ecclesiasticus the question: "Should a man nourish anger against his fellows and expect healing from the LORD? Should a man refuse mercy to his fellows, yet seek pardon for his own sins?" (28:3-4) Go in peace, my child. And pray, trust in God, and cast all your cares on Him, because He cares for you, more than you could ever imagine. Te absolvo de omnibus peccatis tuis in nomine Patris + et Filii et Spiritus Sancti. Amen."

(After seven years of married life in Wisconsin, Rose sees in Milwaukee a billboard that says "Make it Count!") (Flashback of Jack handing her his note saying "Make it count!/ meet me at the clock" and then of Rose meeting him at the clock)

Rose (to Darrell): Honey, may I meet you at the department store in about a half hour? I'd like to look for a few personal things, and it should save us a little time. (She finds the biggest clock in the city, nothing happens, she waits, getting colder and colder, then slumps to the ground, sleeps, has dream of kissing Jack in the cold Atlantic, then saying to him, "I'm not cold anymore!")

Jack: Rose, where there is light, there is warmth…always follow the light, my Rose, always the light.

(She wakes up shivering with Darrell's touch and words…)

Darrell: Rose, are you okay? I've been looking for you for over an hour. How long have you been here?

(He takes her in his arms, still shivering, and leads her away. She looks up at a big light, stops, then…)

Rose: "I'll be okay.

"Every year on the anniversary of the sinking, I thought of Jack more than usual. And on those nights I would usually dream of him. Sometimes I would dream that we were on the Titanic (Show scenes) ….other times I would dream we were in NY (scenes)…or in San Francisco (scenes)…or in Paris (scenes)…. More often, though, I would dream that we were together here in Wisconsin raising the children (scenes).

"On the tenth anniversary of the sinking I had an especially powerful dream. It had been very cold, as it often is in Wisconsin during the winter, and I dreamed that Jack was standing before me. He said, "Follow the light, my Rose, and you will never be cold."

Rose: O Jack, be yourself my light. You're the light I need, Jack!

Jack: Rose, I'm just a little candle, and I was never lit until you and I were together on the bow of the Titanic, flying on the wings of the wind. I've passed beyond, but I will still be with you to help you, especially when you need me the most. But you must go on. Love Darrell and the children. They will be your consolation and your joy. And try to let go of what weighs down your heart… Plant your garden, my dearest.

"When I awoke I knew what I had to do. My heart was the garden he was speaking of, and I had to uproot the weeds of resentment and bitterness I felt toward those I blamed for Jack's death. I tried, I prayed, I confided in Fr. Stachoviac, but it just wouldn't go away.

While my lips could say the words, my heart would still rebel."

(Show other scenes in the life of the Calvert family, including…)

Kendall (Rose's eldest daughter, 9 years old): Mommy, I memorized "The Song of the Silent Swan"! Listen!… (She recites the poem, while her younger sisters and brother look on. Show crucifix on wall, also picture of the Sacred Heart of Jesus next to that of the Immaculate Heart of Mary.)

Rose: Kendall, that was beautiful!

"Jack never spoke to me in a dream again until April 14, 1962, the fiftieth anniversary of the sinking of the Titanic, although I still at times felt his presence, especially when I needed help in some way.

"But long before that, soon after the stock market crash of 1929, I had a terrifying experience. I hadn't heard yet of Caledon committing suicide, but it seemed to me like I woke up in the night seeing him walking into my room, exactly as he did when he gave me the diamond necklace.

(Show same setting as before, same clothing, etc.)

"He was holding the diamond necklace and said…":

Caledon: I was going to wait until the engagement party to give this to you, but now I think that it would be better if I give it to you this special night. (He approaches Rose, puts the necklace on her, as before, then)

Caledon: I always win, Rose. You should know that by now. I *always* win.

(He starts strangling her with the necklace, and after several seconds the chain breaks and Caledon starts choking her from the front. Blood is coming out of his mouth and nose. Rose wakes up screaming, then sobbing.)

"Later that night I dreamed of Jack and I remember waking up feeling at peace, even though the dream of Caledon frightened me beyond description…I would later have other dreams in which it seemed like two forces, one good and one evil, were struggling against each other for possession of me. These were often represented by Jack and Caledon.

Dream 1: Rose riding horse, then a pack of vicious dogs (or hyenas) chases her, trying to bite her, then they are driven off by a lion.

Dream 2: Rose deep sea fishing, catches a large marlin which morphs into a large great white shark when it is close to the boat, then porpoises ram it to death, after which it morphs into Caledon, raging and bleeding out his mouth, nose and the back of his head, after which he sinks into the water.

Dream 3: Rose flying plane, when pterodactyl with Caledon riding it swoops down and damages plane, which plummets. Jack on huge eagle approaches plane, Jack tells Rose to jump so he can save her, she does so after hesitating, and rides double with Jack; then Jack directs eagle to attack Caledon, who falls to earth screaming when pterodactyl is killed.

"I went to see a psychologist about these strange and powerful dreams."

Psychologist: I think there's a good chance that what's causing these dreams is the unresolved tension which remains deep within your psyche on account of your having abandoned Caledon for Jack, and then unfortunately ending up with neither, while you continue to hold on to your feelings for Jack. Plus Caledon having recently died will make these feelings stronger than normal, since both Jack and Caledon are now on, you might say, equal footing, although in a negative way, since both are now dead. When you add this all up, and combine it with your personal beliefs in the afterlife and in the personification of good and evil in God and... Satan or...demons, it all points to a type of conflict resolution taking place within your subconscious.

Rose: What about the dream of Caledon right around the time that he put a gun in his mouth and killed himself, but I hadn't even heard about it yet? And he was bleeding out the mouth in the dream.

Psychologist: Even the dream of Caledon and of him bleeding out the mouth can be traced to the connection in your mind between the stock market crash and the fact that many formerly wealthy people were committing suicide after losing all they had. I wouldn't be too concerned about that. I believe that these dreams will gradually diminish in both intensity and frequency as time goes on. Just as in our bodies, there is also a type of self-corrective mechanism within our psyche, at least within the normal psyche. But if the dreams continue as they are or cause you further disturbance after, say, two months, why don't you give me a call and then we can think about prescribing something to help you to sleep more peacefully.

(Show Fr. Padolano in confessional speaking to Rose behind grill)

Fr. P: It may be that this man with whom you broke off your engagement felt hatred not only for the man you loved but hatred for you as well, for what he may have perceived as an intolerable insult against him. It sometimes happens that when one is consumed by hatred, the person who is hated is *cursed* in some way, which even if it does not involve the explicit or intentional invoking of evil spirits, can lead to demonic assaults of various kinds. This is known as diabolical *oppression*, which is much more common than most people think, as opposed to diabolical *possession*, which is relatively rare. This may very well be the case with your disturbing dream at the time of this man's death. If in fact this man invoked a curse upon you before he killed himself, this could explain what you experienced. Most likely it will not happen again, but it helps of course to arm oneself spiritually against the devil. Do you pray the prayer to St. Michael the archangel daily?

Rose: Usually just at Sunday Mass when the priest says it, but I will pray it daily if you recommend it.

Fr. P: Yes, and I also strongly recommend that you maintain a strong prayer life, including the holy rosary, and receive the sacraments of confession and holy communion frequently. Is there anything else?

Rose: Yes, Father. I still feel bitterness in my heart against those whom I hold responsible for Jack's death, and Jeremy's too, but not as much, even though he was my husband.

Fr. P: Yes, I will pray for you. And if you continue to pray for this grace, you will receive it, I can assure you. Te absolvo de omnibus peccatis tuis + in nomine Patris et Filii et Spiritus Sancti. Amen.

"I never went back to see the psychologist. The violent and fearful dreams did stop, although I would still occasionally dream of Jack. There were never any more words spoken, however, until that day in 1962 on the hundredth anniversary of the sinking. It was then that Jack said, 'It won't be too much longer, my darling, before you will find me. You will come to me on the sea. You will give your heart to me, and it is then that you will also find it.'

"I would never forget those words and I don't think a day has gone by that I have not thought of them and pondered them in my heart.

"There is much that could be written about those intervening years, but as this diary concerns itself primarily with my thoughts, dreams, and experiences relating in some way to Jack, one dream and one experience of Jack's presence and help will suffice here.

"One day back in 1977 I was driving with my granddaughter Lizzy, and she turned on the radio."

 (Show scene: Radio playing "I Can Dream About You [If I Can't Hold You Tonight]". While Rose listens, a tear goes down her cheek, then she flashes back to kissing Jack, then...)

Lizzy: Grandma! Look out!

(Show car over center divider, other car coming almost head on. Suddenly the steering wheel turns on its own, the two cars barely miss each other, Rose's car after several fish-tails is back under control.)

Lizzy: Oh my gosh! That was close! What happened, Grandma? Are you feeling okay?

(Then Rose passes an oncoming car with Jack in it, waving to her. It happens quickly but Rose is pretty sure it was him. She looks in the rear view mirror and whispers, "Jack".

Rose: Oh, I'm so sorry, dear. I think I just...spaced out for a few seconds. That song...it brought back memories...bitter-sweet memories... of long ago.

Lizzy: Was it someone you loved when you were young?

Rose: Yes, dear. Someone I loved very much. Sometimes I think maybe too much. (She smiles)

Lizzy: Well I hope *I* don't love anyone so much that they get me to forget I'm driving a car!

Rose: I hope not too, dear. I hope not too. (She shakes her head, smiling. Lizzy looks at her quizzically.)

"The dream I'll relate was in 1960. (Show dream) I saw Jack standing in front of a church, and there was a sign that said, 'Mary Star of the Sea Catholic Church'. Two years later, when our church here was built, it was given that name, and I had never said a word about the dream to anyone."

(After seeing news story on the Titanic findings: in her bed on the salvage ship that night, sleeping, Rose opens her eyes and sees Jack, who says to her: "Are you ready to come to me, my Rose? Are you ready to let go?"

Rose: Yes, Jack, I'll do anything to be with you!

Jack: I've been looking forward to this moment. All of us have. (He nods to her, smiling, then fades away.)

 (Rose gets out of bed, gets the diamond and walks out of the room stealthily. After dropping the necklace into the sea, Rose, seated in her cabin, turns and sees Jack.)

Jack: How did it feel to let go of the diamond after all these years?

Rose: I felt...free. I've waited a long time to be able to give it to you.

Jack (smiles): Now are you ready to let go of everything?

(Flashback of Rose talking about the selfish Titanic survivors: "… they would wait for an absolution that would never come.")

Rose (crying): It's so hard, Jack….Is that what you want me to do?

Jack: Yes, Rose, that would make me happy…and not just me… all of us…and you too.

Rose: Oh Jack, it hurts too much to think about how they took you from me. We could have been so happy together all these years… They should have come back and saved you, but they only thought of themselves.

Jack: Yes, that's true, but it also allowed me to offer my life for you, that you might go on and become everything you could be and come to this point of letting go. Then your life will be made complete. Just like the swan saving its beautiful song until the day when it dies… I know it's painful, Rose, but sweeter is pleasure after pain. When you gave birth to your children you experienced pain, but after you had given birth you no longer remembered the pain because of the joy you felt when you held them in your arms…You can do it, Rose. I did it; you can do it. I forgave them long ago… It can make us one again. We do it together. I jump, you jump, remember?… You have said that I saved you in every way. (Flashback: "…he saved my life. In fact he saved me in every way that a person can be saved"). That's only partly true, my love. I can help you. But there is one way in which only you can help yourself. Even if we have faith so as to be able to move mountains, but do not have love, we are nothing. If we give away all we have, but do not have love, we gain nothing." (He hands her a sheet of paper, then slowly disappears. Rose looks at it. It is a poem entitled "Love is…". Show title and first several lines. Rose reads the poem to herself. Then show the writing at the bottom of the sheet: "Make it count! / Meet me at the clock." Rose starts crying, holding the sheet to her heart.)

Rose: I'm sorry… I forgive them.…I forgive them …You jump, I jump." (She has tears in her eyes, but looks at peace.)

(Rose writes in diary, then on a separate piece of paper. She looks at her various mementos, closes her eyes with hands folded before her face for several seconds, looks in a mirror and adjusts her hair a bit, then lies down. She looks happy. Show last scene of *Titanic*: meeting Jack at the clock, kissing, clapping, skylight above.)

(Show Lizzy on last page of diary. The last entry says

"Night of her death, 1996")

"This will be my last entry in this diary. It is the request that I be buried here at sea where the Titanic went down. I hope those in authority will not refuse a woman's last request, one who has waited since 1912 to be with the one she loved most, the one she lost here and whom she has kept in her heart these last 84 years."

"Rose Dawson Calvert"

(Lizzy reads a stick 'em note on the last page)

"Dear Lizzy,
If you will go to my little wooden box on the table, you will find a note for you to keep just for yourself. You will see why when you read it."

(She removes stick 'em note, gets note from box and reads it)

"Dear Lizzy,
"The Coeur de Mere should be very close to the Titanic, since in

my clumsiness I dropped it off the side of this salvage ship we're on. You probably shouldn't tell anyone this, though, except maybe the dreamboat you hopefully find soon and marry. If it happens to be Brock, so much the better, since that will make the job a little easier, I imagine. He does seem like a very nice young man, don't you think? But the effort will be worth it, my dear, since we appreciate things more when we work a little bit to acquire them. "Jack left you a little gift to help you remember us. It's on top of my things in the trunk. Also, could you please see to it that Jack's poem 'Love is...' is recited at my funeral? It is also there in the trunk. Thank you, dear."

(Lizzy first finds the poem with "Make it count! / Meet me at the clock" at the bottom of the page, then finds a drawing of Jack and Rose, he standing behind her, with his arms around her, her hands on his. Rose is wearing the diamond necklace.)

(Show coroner finished examining the body)

Coroner: I don't see any sign of drug overdose. It appears she just died in her sleep. At a hundred years old, that's not an unusual way to go.

(Show body being put on helicopter)

Lizzy (to Brock): You don't know how much we appreciate you leaving the ship here until after the funeral.

Brock: It's the least we can do, Lizzy. It also provides me with a good reason to take a look into the back section of the Titanic for a few things during the next few days.

Priest (giving homily at funeral in overflow crowded church): ... and if like the faithful steward in the gospel we have prepared our souls to meet Our Lord, then when that day comes, that day that shall come to us all, we shall also be like him, for we shall see him as he is, and our joy will know no bounds…. I would like to now share something with you about Rose Dawson Calvert. Those of you who were at the rosary service yesterday heard several very moving eulogies about Rose, her so many charitable works done in secret and the many lives she touched with her love, kindness, and overwhelming generosity. This isn't the time to give another eulogy, but I'd like to tell you a few things that Rose made me promise to keep secret while she lived, things that only a handful of people knew, and they have kept it secret as well. Rose inherited a substantial fortune a number of years ago from a woman named Molly Brown, known by many as "the unsinkable Molly Brown", who survived the sinking of the Titanic back in 1912. It has just come to my attention two days ago that Rose also survived the sinking of the Titanic (some gasps and whispering in congregation). She must not have told many people about this. It was only learned by her own family even when they read her diary after she died on a salvage boat in the Atlantic which had in fact found the Titanic several days before and was studying and excavating the ship. Rose died directly over the Titanic, from which she was rescued in 1912… I have not read the diary, so I'm not in a position to talk about it. But I am in a position now to tell you that Rose Dawson Calvert, the feisty old woman who lived a simple life in a small, modest home and was always caring about others to the point of neglecting herself, and almost never spoke about herself, except to maybe blame herself for something, this humble woman who loved God and loved her neighbor with her whole heart, contributed millions of dollars to the poor, the homeless, the infirm and the needy here in Wisconsin and throughout the world. She was the anonymous donor who back in 1962 built this church. She built Good Samaritan House in Milwaukee for those suffering and dying of Aids. I could go on and on talking about her generous support of all those in need in any way, from homeless shelters and soup kitchens to crisis pregnancy shelters for women. One time I tried to urge her to do a little something for herself, buy a nicer house, take a nice vacation somewhere. And I'll never forget her reply. She said, "Father, The Lord God has blessed me in so many ways. I have everything I need in this world. There are countless other who don't." Another time I asked her what inspired her to so generously support so many worthy causes. She said, "Since you ask me, Father, I will go home and write down the answer to that question, but on the condition that you tell no one while I'm still living." This was seven years ago. And I have here in my hand what she wrote… (Show Rose writing at her desk)

Rose: "I write this at the request of Fr. Phillip O'Donnell and respectfully request that its contents not be revealed until after my death.

"I have been asked what has inspired me to support throughout the years, especially financially, the various worthy causes that I have been blessed to be able to help in what way I could. It would require more than a book to adequately answer that question, but at least one chapter of that unwritten book is in the possession of my dear children and grandchildren and great and great-great grandchildren. In it I tell how I was rescued from death and given new life after the sinking of the Titanic. I was seventeen at the time and two days before the sinking I met a young man named Jack Dawson. I fell in love with him, but I must admit that he fell in love with me first (Show priest and some of congregation trying to hold back a laugh, some with tears in their eyes). We met in the evening at the stern of the ship when I was contemplating suicide. I was ready to jump but he persuaded me not to. During the brief time we were together before the ship went down, Jack not only gave me new hope and a new reason to live, but he gave me much more, more than I can ever express in words. When we were in the water together he pushed me up onto a floating door panel and held onto my hand until the icy water took the last breath from his lungs. I later met Jack's relatives in Chippewa Falls, Wisconsin, married his cousin Jeremy and became a Catholic, which at that time was pretty much a given, unless one was tougher than nails and was ready to weather an almost continuous bombardment of missionary zeal in ten thousand forms from all sides! (laughter) But I changed from an agnostic Episcopalian to Catholic not just because Jeremy was Catholic, but mainly because of the love and the joy I witnessed in the Dawson family, a love and a joy that they passed on to me. What I saw in them was love in action and not just love in words or dreams, and it was in them and through them that I caught a glimpse of what made the man who saved my life who he was, and inspired him to do what he did. So to answer the question, What inspired me to help others in need, it was first Jack Dawson and then his relatives, especially Jeremy and his mother Millie, to whom I was greatly attached and who was like a real mother to me, God rest her sweet soul. What continued to inspire me after that were the words of the gospel, especially the Sermon on the Mount, and also the other scriptures, then the lives and the writings of the saints, then people like Mahatma Gandhi, Dorothy Day, and Mother Teresa of Calcutta. All of them and many more have been my inspiration, including those whose lives have been affected by what little I have been able to do. But behind them all was a voice within my heart, a voice urging me to never give up, to never lose hope, and to give of myself to others without counting the cost and without expecting any reward in this life, to love others as God, especially through others, has always so generously loved me; a voice telling me that I will discover my true self and truly fulfill myself only through a sincere giving of myself to others. And I've always believed that that voice in my heart all these many years was the voice of the young man who died on April 14, 1912, in his heroic and self-sacrificing attempt to save my life... I love you, Jack. And I thank you with all my heart. You gave me so much more than any one - in this world at least - could ever imagine.

"Let me close this note with one of the poems Jack wrote a little over a year before he died. It taught me much about love and also about Jack. It's based on St Paul's teaching on what love consists of. I hardly admit to living up to what it says, but I believe in it with all my heart:

Love is …

Love is patient, love is kind;
All selfish ways it leaves behind.
Love is never harsh or rude;
It governs every changing mood.
Love is generous in giving,
Bears all things and is forgiving.
Love is trusting, never jealous;
For God and neighbor it is zealous.
Love that's true will never fail;
It's always new, it's never stale.
Love dispels all hateful wrath;
It takes the peaceful, gentle path.
Love will never put on airs;
With joy it serves; it always cares.
With love one never seeks oneself:
In giving, it draws down God's wealth.
Love that's true is always pure:
Thus blessed by God, it shall endure.
Love is strong and persevering,
Ever faithful, never fearing.
Love is patient, love is kind;
With love, God's kingdom you shall find.
Nov., 1910

'Greater love than this no man has, than that he lay down is life for others'."

(Show teary-eyed congregation, then hearse leaving parking lot, then sign with name of the church: "Mary Star of the Sea Catholic Church.")

(Some family members and friends arrive on salvage platform in helicopters, others in boats. Catholic burial ceremony, wrapped body lowered into sea above Titanic.)

Child: How long does it take to get to the bottom?

Brock: Well, it's over 10,000 feet deep here or about 2 miles. That means she'll be on the bottom and pretty close to the Titanic in about 20 minutes or so. (Some people wait and are chatting. After about 30 minutes a great rush of bubbles comes up to the surface of the water, continuing for about 30 seconds. All present gasp in amazement, some hug each other with tears in their eyes.)

Brock: This is unbelievable! I can't imagine what would do that!

Lizzy: I have grandma's diary that I can show you. Once you read it you may have some idea what did it.

(That evening, the two are looking out at sea, still on the salvage ship.)

Brock: I wouldn't believe some of the things your grandmother wrote if I didn't see what I saw this afternoon. I thought she could have brought the note and the drawing with her when she came here with you. But if you put it all together, you just have to say…I believe it. Rose Dawson Calvert is definitely the most incredible woman I've ever met in my entire life!

Lizzy: Well, I have to tell you a little secret.

Brock: Oh boy, what next?!

Lizzy: It's nothing strange, just that she told me that she liked you… But, then again, I guess you might be able to call that strange. (They both laugh.)

Brock: That means a lot to me, Lizzy…more than you can imagine.

Lizzy: You know, for a long time now, I've always trusted grandma Rose's judgment. She's usually right on target…And I think she is this time too…I like you too, Brock.
(They look into each other's eyes for a few seconds, smiling.)

Brock: And I like you too.

(They kiss.)

Brock: This is just amazing how all this is happening!

(Show shooting star above couple.)

Lizzy: Look - a shooting star!

(They kiss again)

(Camera raises up above the couple to the stars.)

(Eighteen years later: Brock, Lizzy and four children enter the "Titanic Memorial Museum" in New York.)

Brock: I wonder what new additions they've put in this year.

 Daughter: Dad, what do you say, after this year we start coming here just every *two* years.

 Other daughter: I vote for every *ten*. Then maybe we'll have a better chance of not getting mugged in New York one of these times.

Brock: Almost nobody ever gets mugged where we go, dear. And even downtown New York is a lot safer than it used to be.

Lizzy (puts her arm around daughter): There will always be some danger wherever you go in life, dear. And there are some things you just have to do without fear of the danger involved. You just have to do them because they're the right things to do… Just like there are some things you just can't put a price on.

(They go immediately to a distant section.)

Daughter 1: I hope she doesn't cry.

Daughter 2: She always cries when she sees that picture.

(They stop, Lizzy in front. She smiles, and a tear rolls down her cheek. Show oil painting of the drawing Jack handed Rose the night of her death. Underneath it says, "This painting of Jack Dawson and Rose Dawson Calvert is a reproduction of an original drawing in pencil by Jack Dawson. Jack died in the process of saving Rose's life after the sinking of the Titanic. The original drawing, a cherished heirloom of the Calvert Family, is the only known likeness in existence of the heroic young man.")

Son: Is it okay if we go see the 3-D Titanic show?

Brock: That's fine. We'll meet you there in a little bit.

Daughter 2: Dad, could you get me a necklace like that for my birthday or Christmas?

Brock: That's asking for a lot if you're looking for the real thing.

Daughter, walking away: Of course I want the real thing!

(Brock puts his arms around Lizzy, just as Jack in the painting, as they look at it.)

Brock: You know, you and Rose certainly have a lot in common.

(Lizzy pulls diamond necklace out from under her V-neck sweater and looks down at it briefly as she holds it.)

Lizzy: I don't know. I doubt if *anyone* could be like her.

Brock: Yeah....You know, sometimes I wonder if we should ever tell the kids at all about the necklace. Especially with four of them, and *two* girls.

Lizzy: I wonder what grandma Rose would do?

Brock: We know what *she* would do, because she already did it! And it took me three damn years afterward to find the thing! (They both laugh.)

Lizzy: Gosh...do you think we should?

Brock: Back in the water?

Lizzy (smiling): Back in the water! (They laugh as they look at the painting. Show painting from behind the couple, then zoom in on diamond in painting, then back out showing the live Jack and Rose in that embrace, then she puts her arms out, he does the same, his hands on hers, as wind blows into their faces as on bow of Titanic; she says, "I'm flying, Jack!", then turns her head toward his. They kiss. Play song: "My Heart Will Go On" by Celine Dion (or same melody with different lyrics.)

Other music: Enya

[Alternative story: Molly Brown contacts Jack's relatives and tells
them she met Jack on the Titanic. Since he wasn't on the list of
passengers, Molly telegraphs Chippewa Falls to inform them of his
death, then arranges trip there, along with Rose, to meet family.
(Then make necessary adjustments.)]

[Alternative story 2: Jeremy is killed before the wedding takes
place. Molly comes out for the wedding of Rose and Darrell
Calvert, conversing with a different priest at the reception, etc.]

Made in the USA
Lexington, KY
03 October 2016